Dear Parent:

Here's the race to beat all races!

There's nothing more fun than challenging one's siblings or friends. Whether it's kick-the-can, running the three-legged race, or sailing a boat, healthy competition can make play fun. It makes you work harder and want to do the very best. It doesn't really matter who wins, but it does matter that the play is fair.

Sometimes, as in *Mouse & Mole's Great Race,* one of the players is not always fair. That's where the trouble begins. In families, it can stem from what psychologists call sibling rivalry. Look at how Rat cheats in order to win the boat race. He'll do anything to be considered the best. As in this story, justice usually wins—either through the simple logic of events or through the intervention of a wise adult.

So, here it is, a story for the whole family. It's an exciting tale about a sailboat race. Plus, it may provoke some interesting discussion about ethics. On your mark, get set, GO!!

Sincerely,

Elizabeth Isele
Executive Editor
Weekly Reader Books

Weekly Reader Children's Book Club Presents

MOUSE and MOLE'S GREAT RACE

Diane Redfield Massie

Field Publications
MIDDLETOWN, CT

This book is a presentation of Weekly
Reader Books. Weekly Reader Books
offers book clubs for children from
preschool through high school. For
further information write to: **Weekly
Reader Books,** 4343 Equity Drive,
Columbus, Ohio 43228.

Weekly Reader is a federally registered
trademark of Field Publications.
Printed in the United States of America.

for Marion Haskell Redfield

Mouse hurried down her front steps.
She could see Mole next door, digging
in his garden. "Mole! Mole!" She ran
through the asters at the end of her yard.
"There's going to be a race, Mole, a great
race on the pond!"

Mole spaded carefully around a weed
and rubbed his tired eyes.

"The winner gets a prize!" said Mouse, hopping on one foot.

"Oh?" said Mole. "A prize?" He picked up a stone and planted it carefully next to his squash plant.

"The first one to sail across the pond, wins!" said Mouse. "I'm in the race!"

"Where's your boat?" asked Mole.

"I don't have one yet. I'm going to *build* one. Do you know anything about shipbuilding, Mole?"

Mole thought a moment. He shook his packet of squash seeds and shaded his small, weak eyes. He knew about seeds and digging and plants, so why not boats? "A little," he said.

"Good!" said Mouse. "I can use your help. Rat is making his boat already. He won't let anyone see it."

"Why not?" asked Mole.

"He doesn't want us to copy it. It's going to have three sails."

"How do you know?" asked Mole.

"Rat said so." Mouse looked worriedly toward Rat's yard, beyond the water-lily beds.

They could hear pounding.

"Rat said it's going to be a clipper ship . . . 'the fastest boat on the seas.' That's what Rat said," said Mouse.

"Rat is always bragging," sighed Mole.

"Rat is the only one in the race so far," said Mouse, "except for *me*, of course."

"They all know *I'm* going to win," said Rat, looking through the bushes.

"Rat!" cried Mouse. "We thought you were pounding in your yard."

"That's Heron pounding," said Rat. "She's the navigator."

"Mole's *my* navigator," said Mouse.

"I am?" said Mole. "What's a navigator?"

"They design ships," said Mouse.

"Navigators *navigate* boats," said Rat. "That *means* they make sure the boat is going in the right direction."

"Oh," said Mouse.

"You wouldn't want to sail backwards," said Mole. "Or sideways," he added.

"Mole designs ships," said Mouse.

Rat smiled thinly. His yellow teeth glittered behind his whiskers. "How *many* have you designed?" he asked.

"I forget," said Mole.

"How many sails is your ship going to have?"
asked Rat. He snickered behind his paw.

"One," said Mouse.

"Five," said Mole.

"FIVE sails?!!" Rat laughed. He stepped
on Mole's squash plant and hopped through the ferns.
"It'll never get out of the harbor," he called.

They could see the cattails shake as Rat made
his way home.

"*Five* sails?" said Mouse.

"I was only kidding," said Mole. "Let's get started."

They spent the day collecting things.

Pheasant had a large packing box which she didn't need.

"Good lumber for the deck!" said Mouse.

Mole pushed it into the pond. "We'll float it home."

"I hope you win," called Pheasant, shaking her apron. "Try Turtle down the lane. He might have something useful."

Turtle brought out an old awning from behind his tool shed. It had blue and yellow stripes.

"It's perfect for the sails!" cried Mole.

"It's got thirteen holes where the rain comes in," said Turtle. "Good luck."

"We can mend the holes," said Mouse. "Mole, are you good at sewing?"

"Probably," said Mole.

The frogs in the lilies knew where there was some rope. "Left in the weeds by somebody," they croaked. "You can have it all."

Mouse wound it up on a stick and carried it home.

They spent the rest of the week pounding, and lashing, and sewing.

"Do you think three-boards thick is enough for the deck, Mole?" Mouse walked about, tapping the nails on the bow. She watched Mole fasten the sail to the mast. "It looks more like a *raft* than a boat," she said, doubtfully.

"It's a sailing raft," said Mole. "They're probably the fastest kind."

"Do you think so?"

"Faster than oil barges," said Mole.

Rat's nose poked out of the ferns. "What's *that*, a fly trap?" he said.

"It's our boat," said Mouse.

"BOAT?!!" snorted Rat.

"Heron! Get a look at the fly trap!"

Heron flew over their heads, flapping her great grey wings.

They could hear her hissing laugh as she sailed over the water.

"The race is tomorrow," said Rat. "My ship will be across the pond before that flytrap has a chance to sink."

"SINK?!!" cried Mole, smacking the mast with his paw.

The sail broke loose and slid down the pole. It fell over their heads in a heap. They could hear Rat laughing and clapping his paws outside.

"Let's wait until he leaves," whispered Mouse.

They could see the stripes faintly in the darkness, yellow and blue . . . yellow and blue. There was one tiny hole which Mole had forgotten to mend.

At last the great day arrived.
Crowds were already gathering across the pond.

Mouse could see the frogs on the grandstand.
They were leaping over the seats. "Mole! Mole!"
she called.

Mole was out in his garden, chewing on celery
roots. "I'm having breakfast," he said.

"Hurry, Mole. They're getting ready over
there!" Mouse pulled on the rope at the front of
the raft. It slid easily over the grass. "It's
sliding down the bank!" called Mouse, running after it.
"It's going down to the beach!"

"Wait for me!" yelled Mole. He ran after Mouse
through the lilies, down the reedy bank.

"What if it sinks?" said Mouse. "What if . . . ,"
and she stopped.

There, at the edge of the water, stood Rat's
ship. It had three big sails, and a flag at the
bow, and there was even a deck chair in front.

"It's Rat's ship," whispered Mouse.

Mole stared. His mouth felt dry, and his paws
felt damp. The letters on the bow were gold. They
said, "R A T." He leaned against the raft. It
slid on the sand and Mole fell into the pond. SPLASH!

"LOOK, MOLE!" cried Mouse. "Our raft is FLOATING!"

Mole shook the water from his whiskers and dried his eyes with his paws. "I knew it would," he said.

They climbed on board and unfastened the sail.

"ATTENTION!" called someone from across the pond. Three pheasants sat in the judges' seats. They waved their megaphones. "ATTENTION! THE GREAT RACE IS ABOUT TO BEGIN! Will the contestants please take their places!"

Mole pulled on the rope to the sail, and the wind blew them slowly along the bank, away from Rat's ship.

"We're going in the wrong direction, Mole!" said Mouse.

"I can't help it!" said Mole. "It *wants* to go over here!"

"We're going toward the lily beds!" cried Mouse.

"Help!" yelled Mole. "The wind's wrong!"

"Mole," said Mouse, "are you sure you know how to sail?"

"We can *pull* it over there!" cried Mole. "It's the only way!" He jumped off in the shallow water and waded to shore, pulling the raft after him. He pulled it up next to Rat's ship.

"Well, look who's here," said Rat from above, standing on his deck chair. "It's the flytrap! HA! HA! HA!"

Heron sat in the back of Rat's ship. She ruffled her feathers crossly under the red and black sails.

"When you hear the gun," called the judges, "set sail! And may the best ship win!"
Everyone clapped and cheered.

BANG! went the gun from across the pond.

"WE'RE OFF!" yelled Rat. "SHIP AHOY!"

The great ship moved out, away from shore.
It sailed between the lily beds toward open water.

"They're ahead of us!" cried Mouse.

Mole pulled on the sail. It caught the breeze
like a thistle seed, and the raft began to move.

"We're sailing!" yelled Mole. "We're sailing!"

Everyone cheered across the pond. "Come on,
Mouse and Mole!"

Rat's ship was still ahead. It glided past
the cattails.

"Come on wind!" yelled Mole.

"LOOK OUT!" shouted Mouse. "We're heading into the cattail beds! Starboard side, Mole!"

Mole ran to the other side, pulling the sail after him. It fluttered and flapped and then hung down like a moth that had gone to sleep.

"WHAT HAPPENED?" cried Mouse.

The raft drifted slowly into the cattails.

"The wind's stopped," said Mole.

They watched Rat's ship sail straight ahead. It docked at the grandstand pier.

"They've won," said Mouse, sadly.

Mole wiped his nose on his sleeve.

"THE WINNER," announced the judge, "IS RAT'S SHIP!"

Everyone clapped.

Rat jumped off onto the pier. He bowed and waved. "What's the prize?" he asked.

"A ship's bell, six deck chairs, and a clock," said one of the judges.

"All for ME!" shouted Rat.

"We'll divide them," said Heron, "like you said."

"You can't divide a clock!" said Rat.

"*You* can have the clock and I'll have the bell," said Heron, "and *three* deck chairs!"

"They're *all* mine!" yelled Rat.

"I might have known," cried Heron, "and after all my help!" She stood up, pulling out her long, yellow legs. Lily stems hung from her toes.

"WAIT!" cried Rat. "DON'T LEAVE!"

But Heron flapped her great long wings and flew off over the pond.

Bubble bubble bubble, went Rat's ship. Bubble bubble bubble. It sank slowly into the pond.

"GOOD HEAVENS!" cried the judges. "LOOK AT RAT'S SHIP!"

"It's sitting on the bottom!"
said one.

"What are those two big holes
in the deck at the back?!!" said another.
"They go all the way through!"

The judges looked at each other. They examined
the holes in Rat's deck.

"How strange!"
whispered the frogs.

Rat gathered up the bell.
"I'll need some help with the chairs
and clock," he said.

"WAIT!" cried the judges through their
megaphones. "RAT'S SHIP IS A FAKE!"

"A FAKE?" said the frogs,
falling back on their seats. "A FAKE?!!" said Turtle
to Pheasant.

Rat disappeared behind the lilies, dropping
the bell in the grass.

"Rat's ship did not *sail* across the pond,"
announced the first Judge. "It walked!"

"W A L K E D?" the frogs stared at each other.

"Heron's legs went through to the bottom.
She *walked* the ship across."

"NO!" gasped the frogs.

"LOOK!" cried Turtle, jumping up.
"There are Mouse and Mole coming out of the cattails!
They're sailing again!"

"HERE THEY COME!" shouted Pheasant.

Everyone cheered.

Mole held onto the rope as they sailed past
the pier.

"SHIP AHOY!" yelled Mouse.

The raft slid up on the sand next to the
cheering crowd.

"ATTENTION!" announced the judges.
"We have a correction to make.
THE WINNER OF THE GREAT RACE . . .
IS MOUSE AND MOLE'S SHIP!
THE FIRST SHIP TO *SAIL* ACROSS THE POND!"

"Y E E E E A A A A A A A A Y!" yelled everyone.
Mouse and Mole bowed.

Pheasant brought out some mulberry punch
and plenty of raisin tarts.

"Would you rather have the bell and three
chairs, or the clock and three chairs?"
whispered Mouse, as Pheasant filled their cups.

Mole drank a sip from his punch. "What would
you rather have?"

"I like the bell," said Mouse, chewing on
a tart.

"I was hoping you'd say that," whispered Mole.
He picked up the clock and listened to it tick.
"It's nice to know how many carrot roots you can
eat in a minute," he said. "Things like that."

Mouse smiled. "We'll sit in our chairs in
the garden," she said. "I mean, when we aren't
sailing."